D1588071

A Note to Parents and Caregivers:

Read-it! Readers are for children who are just starting on the amazing road to reading. These beautiful books support both the acquisition of reading skills and the love of books.

The RED LEVEL presents familiar topics using common words and repeating sentence patterns.

The BLUE LEVEL presents new ideas using a larger vocabulary and varied sentence structure.

The YELLOW LEVEL presents more challenging ideas, a broad vocabulary, and wide variety in sentence structure.

The GREEN LEVEL presents more complex ideas, an extended vocabulary range, and expanded language structures.

When sharing a book with your child, read in short stretches, pausing often to talk about the pictures. Have your child turn the pages and point to the pictures and familiar words. And be sure to reread favorite stories or parts of stories.

There is no right or wrong way to share books with children. Find time to read with your child, and pass on the legacy of literacy.

Adria F. Klein, Ph.D.
Professor Emeritus
California State University
San Bernardino, California

Managing Editors: Bob Temple, Catherine Neitge
Creative Director: Terri Foley
Editor: Jerry Ruff
Editorial Adviser: Mary Lindeen
Designer: Melissa Kes
Page production: Picture Window Books
The illustrations in this book were rendered digitally.

Picture Window Books
5115 Excelsior Boulevard
Suite 232
Minneapolis, MN 55416
877-845-8392
www.picturewindowbooks.com

Copyright © 2005 by Picture Window Books
All rights reserved. No part of this book may be reproduced without written
permission from the publisher. The publisher takes no responsibility for the use of
any of the materials or methods described in this book, nor for the products thereof.

Printed in the United States of America.

Library of Congress Cataloging-in-Publication Data
Blair, Eric.
Tom Thumb: a retelling of the classic fairy tale / by Eric Blair; illustrated by
Todd Ouren.
p. cm. — (Read-it! readers fairy tales)
Summary: A boy the size of his father's thumb has a series of adventures, including
stopping a pair of thieves, being swallowed by a cow, and tricking a wolf into bringing
him back home.
ISBN 1-4048-0593-1 (reinforced library binding: alk. paper)
[1. Fairy tales. 2. Folklore—England.] I. Ouren, Todd, ill. II. Tom Thumb. English.
III. Title. IV. Series.
PZ8.B5688Tom 2004
398.2—dc22   2003028246

Tom Thumb

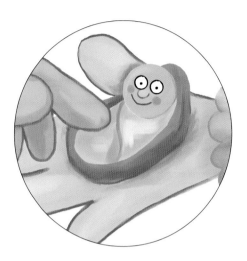

By Eric Blair
Illustrated by Todd Ouren

Special thanks to our advisers for their expertise:
Adria F. Klein, Ph.D.
Professor Emeritus, California State University
San Bernardino, California

Kathleen Baxter, M.A.
Former Coordinator of Children's Services
Anoka County (Minnesota) Library

Susan Kesselring, M.A.
Literacy Educator
Rosemount-Apple Valley-Eagan (Minnesota) School District

PICTURE WINDOW BOOKS
Minneapolis, Minnesota

Once upon a time, there was a poor woodcutter who had no children. "I'd love to have a child," he said, "even if he were as small as a thumb."

Soon after, the woodcutter and his wife had a baby boy. He was no bigger than a thumb, so his parents called him Tom Thumb.

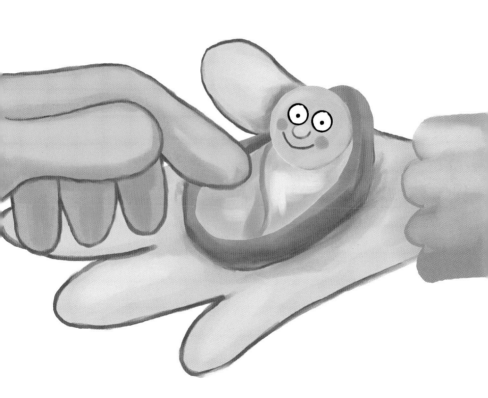

One day, Tom's father went into the forest. "I wish someone could bring the cart," he said.
"I can do that," said Tom.
His father laughed. "You are too small."

With that, Tom leaped into the horse's ear and began to give commands.

Tom and his cart came around a corner where two men stood. "I see a cart, and I hear the driver," said one, "but I can't see him." The men decided to follow the cart.

When he came to the spot in the forest where his father was working, Tom called out to him.

The woodcutter took his son out of the horse's ear and placed him on the ground. The strangers were watching.

The strangers were amazed to see the tiny boy. "We could make a fortune with such a little man," said one. "Let's buy him."

The strangers went to the woodcutter.
"Sell us the little man," one of
them said.

Tom crawled up to his father's collar and whispered, "Take the money. I will escape and be home in time for dinner."

Tom's father sold him to the strangers. Tom rode away on the brim of one stranger's hat.

Before long, Tom cried, "Set me down for a moment. I have to do something."

When the stranger put him down,

Tom ran into a mouse hole.

The strangers could not find him.

At dusk, two thieves came by.

"How can we get the money?" Tom heard one thief ask.

"I will help you!" Tom cried.

Tom came out of the mouse hole. The thieves scooped him up. They took him to the house they wanted to rob.

Tom crawled through the window, but he did not steal any money. Instead, he yelled, "Do you want all of it?" "Be quiet!" whispered the thieves. "You will wake everyone. Just bring us the money."

"Whatever you want!" Tom shouted.
At this, the maid woke up and
stumbled in. The thieves ran off, and
Tom crept away to the barn.

The next morning, the maid got up to feed the cows. She grabbed the pile of hay in which Tom was sleeping. The cow ate the hay, and Tom slid down into the cow's stomach.

"Help!" Tom cried. The maid was shocked to hear the cow speak. She decided the cow should be butchered at once.

Tom fell out of the cow, and the butcher threw him aside. Soon, a hungry wolf came by and ate Tom whole.

Tom wasn't afraid. He had a plan. "Dear wolf, I know where you can find a meal!" he shouted. Tom described the way to his father's house.

When the wolf arrived at Tom's house, he slipped into the pantry.

He found plenty of food.

After the wolf had eaten, he was so fat, he couldn't get out of the pantry.

Tom screamed as loud as he could. Tom's father and mother were sleeping in the next room. His screams woke them. They ran to the pantry.

27

Tom's father wanted to kill the wolf.
Just then, Tom cried, "It's me! Your
little Tom! I'm in the wolf's belly.
Please get me out."

Tom's parents killed the wolf and pulled out their son. They were overjoyed to have him home.

"I've had some adventures," said Tom. "I've been in a mouse hole, a barn, a cow's stomach, and a wolf's stomach. Now that I'm home, I'm never going away again."

"And we'll never sell you again," said Tom's father. "Not for all the gold in the world."

Levels for *Read-it!* Readers

Read-it! Readers help children practice early reading
skills with brightly illustrated stories.

Red Level: Familiar topics with frequently used words and
repeating patterns.

Blue Level: New ideas with a larger vocabulary and a variety
of language structures.

Little Red Riding Hood by Maggie Moore
The Three Little Pigs by Maggie Moore

Yellow Level: Challenging ideas with an expanded vocabulary
and a wide variety of sentences.

Cinderella by Barrie Wade
Goldilocks and the Three Bears by Barrie Wade
Jack and the Beanstalk by Maggie Moore
The Three Billy Goats Gruff by Barrie Wade

Green Level: More complex ideas with an extended vocabulary
range and expanded language structures.

The Brave Little Tailor by Eric Blair
The Bremen Town Musicians by Eric Blair
The Emperor's New Clothes by Susan Blackaby
The Fisherman and His Wife by Eric Blair
The Frog Prince by Eric Blair
Hansel and Gretel by Eric Blair
The Little Mermaid by Susan Blackaby
The Princess and the Pea by Susan Blackaby
Puss in Boots by Eric Blair
Rumpelstiltskin by Eric Blair
The Shoemaker and His Elves by Eric Blair
Snow White by Eric Blair
Sleeping Beauty by Eric Blair
The Steadfast Tin Soldier by Susan Blackaby
Thumbelina by Susan Blackaby
Tom Thumb by Eric Blair
The Ugly Duckling by Susan Blackaby
The Wolf and the Seven Little Kids by Eric Blair

**A complete list of *Read-it!* Readers is available on our Web site:
www.picturewindowbooks.com**